Fairy Magic
Color by Number
BLACK BACKGROUND
An Enchanted Mosaic
Coloring Book For Adults
Mosaic Coloring Books for Adults by Number

Thank you
for your purchase!

Claim your FREE digital copy of our
Highlight Reel Color By Number Book:

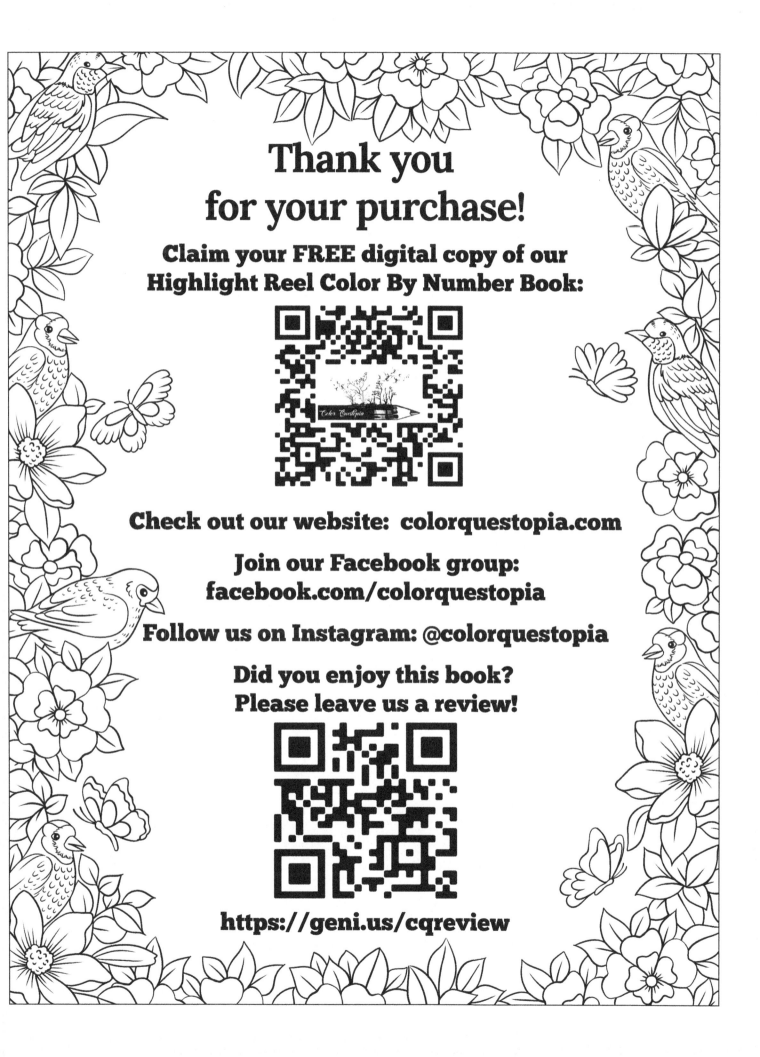

Check out our website: colorquestopia.com

Join our Facebook group:
facebook.com/colorquestopia

Follow us on Instagram: @colorquestopia

Did you enjoy this book?
Please leave us a review!

https://geni.us/cqreview

Color By Number Tips

1. **Relax and have fun**
   Let your cares slip away as you color the images. Take your time. Coloring is a meditative activity and there's no wrong way to do it. Feel free to color as you listen to music, watch TV, lounge in bed- do whatever relaxes you most! You can also color while you're out and about- on the train or at a cafe- take the book with you anywhere you go. Coloring is therapeutic and is great for stress relief and relaxation!

2. **Colors corresponding to each number are shown on the back cover of the book**
   Each number corresponds to a color shown on the back of the book. You can match the color as closely as you like- but feel free to change the color or the shade if you don't have the exact color match- that's totally fine. Although this is a color by number book, it's completely okay to get creative and color the images with whichever colors you like and have. The numbers are there to be a guide and to allow you to color without having to focus your energy on choosing colors.

3. **Choose your coloring tools**
   Everyone has their favorite coloring markers, crayons, pencils, pens- even paints! Feel free to color with any tool that you like! If you choose markers or paints, we recommend putting a blank sheet of paper or cardboard behind each image, so that your colors don't run onto the next image.

   Enjoy!

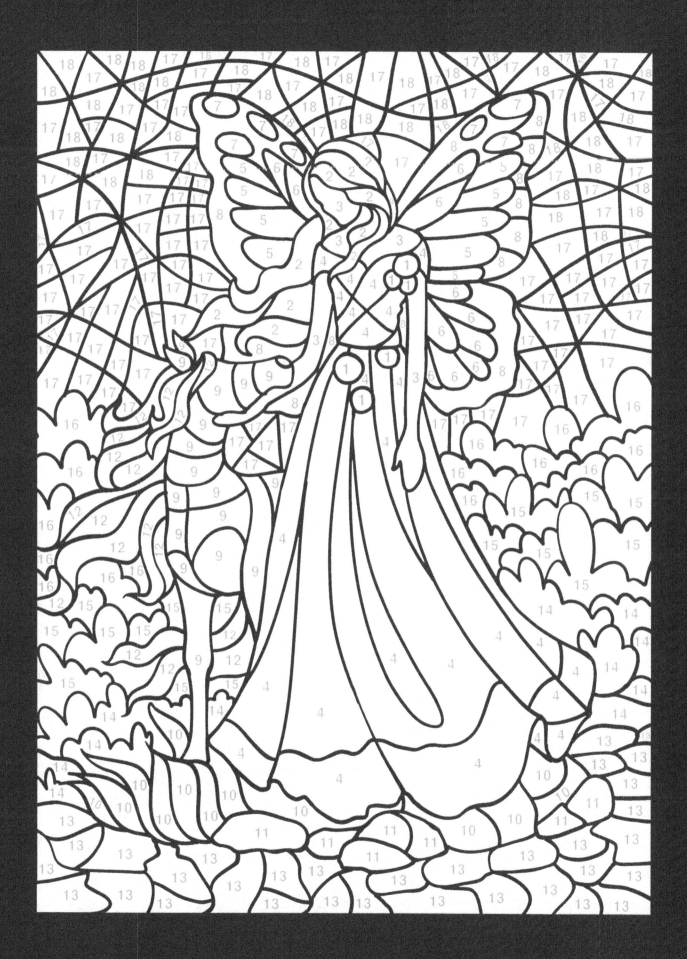

1. Peach
2. Dark Brown
3. Light Orange
4. Violet
5. Brown
6. Yellow
7. Red
8. Dark Red
9. Green
10. Light Green
11. Orange
12. Dark Green
13. Light Brown
14. Army Green
15. Light Pink
16. Neon Green
17. Light Blue
18. Light Gray

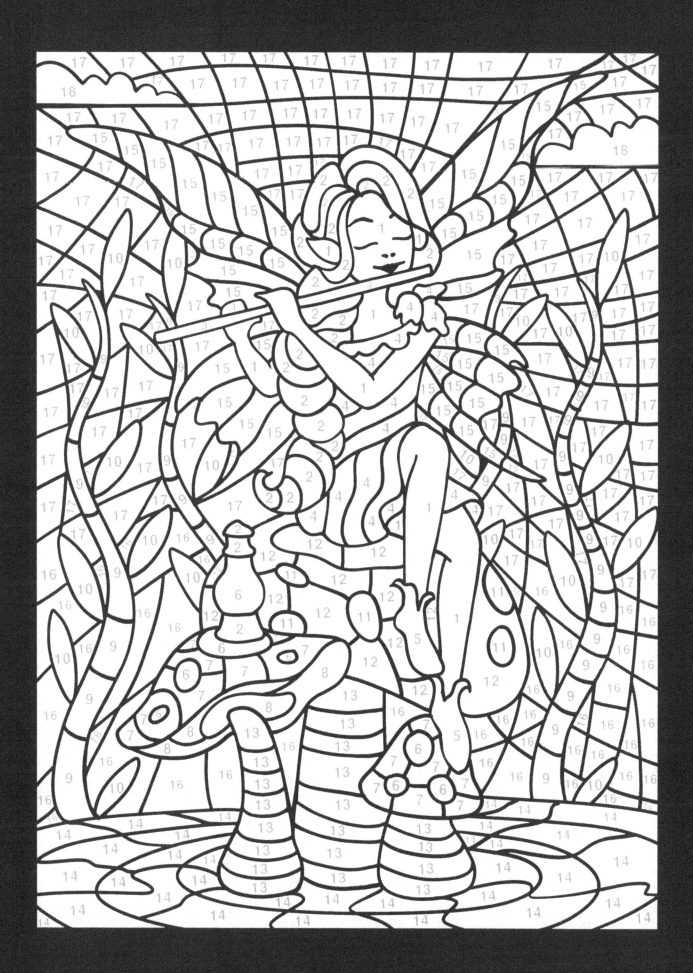

1. Peach
2. Blue
3. Light Pink
4. Pink
5. Dark Brown
6. Violet
7. Yellow
8. Baby Blue
9. Light Blue
10. Light Gray
11. Neon Green
12. Army Green
13. Dark Green
14. Green
15. Light Green
16. Red
17. Orange

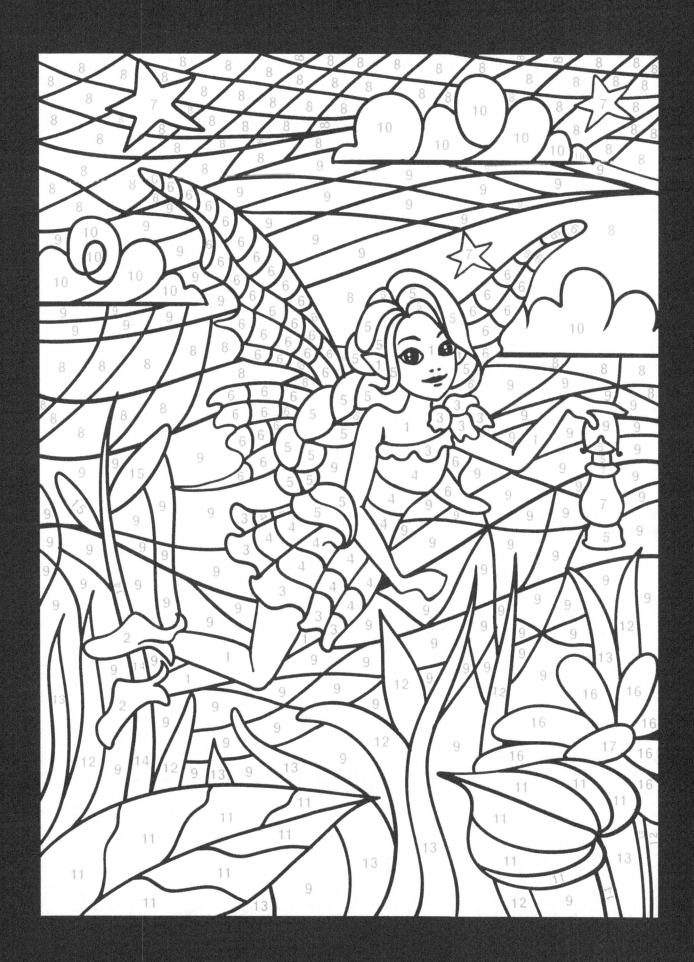

1. Peach
2. Orange
3. Blue
4. Dark Brown
5. Light Pink
6. Brown
7. Light Brown
8. Light Blue
9. Green
10. Light Orange
11. Red
12. Yellow
13. Dark Green
14. Army Green
15. Light Green
16. Medium Green
17. Neon Green

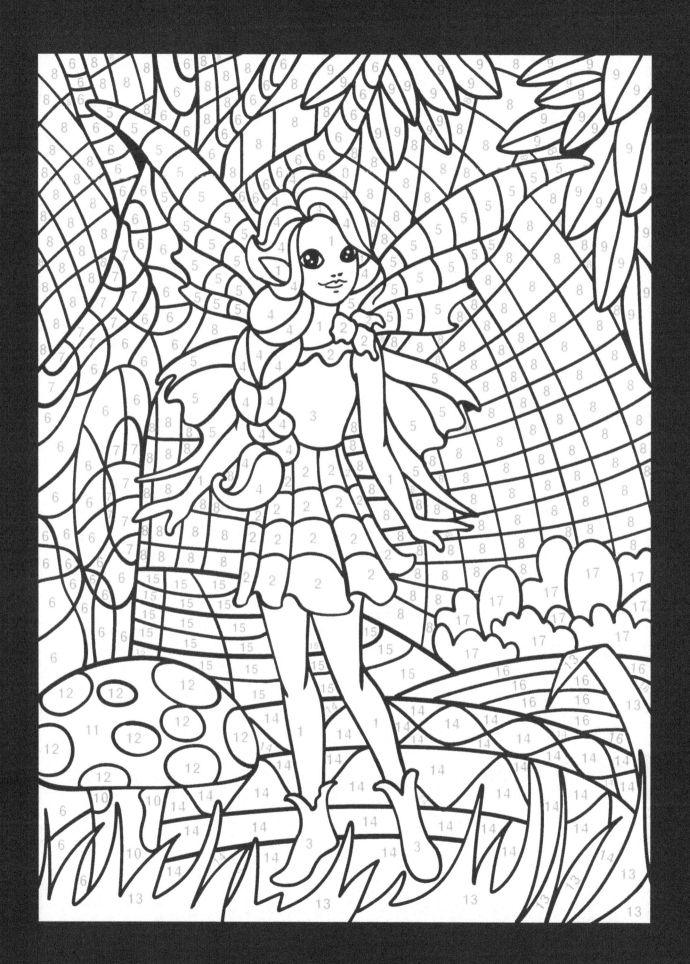

1. Yellow
2. Neon Green
3. Dark Brown
4. Peach
5. Blue
6. Pink
7. Orange
8. Red
9. Light Orange
10. Gray
11. Dark Green
12. Dark Gray
13. Green
14. Medium Green
15. Light Green
16. Light Blue
17. Baby Blue

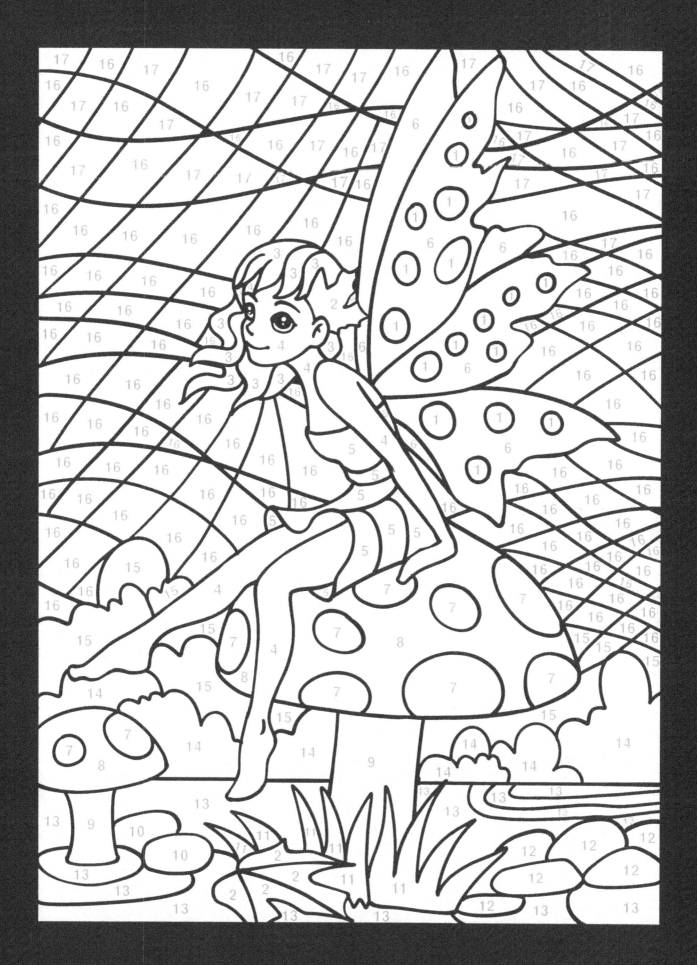

1. Dark Brown
2. Peach
3. Yellow
4. Pink
5. Light Pink
6. Light Blue
7. Baby Blue
8. Red
9. Light Orange
10. Army Green
11. Green
12. Light Green
13. Neon Green
14. Orange
15. Blue

16. Dark Green
17. Medium Green

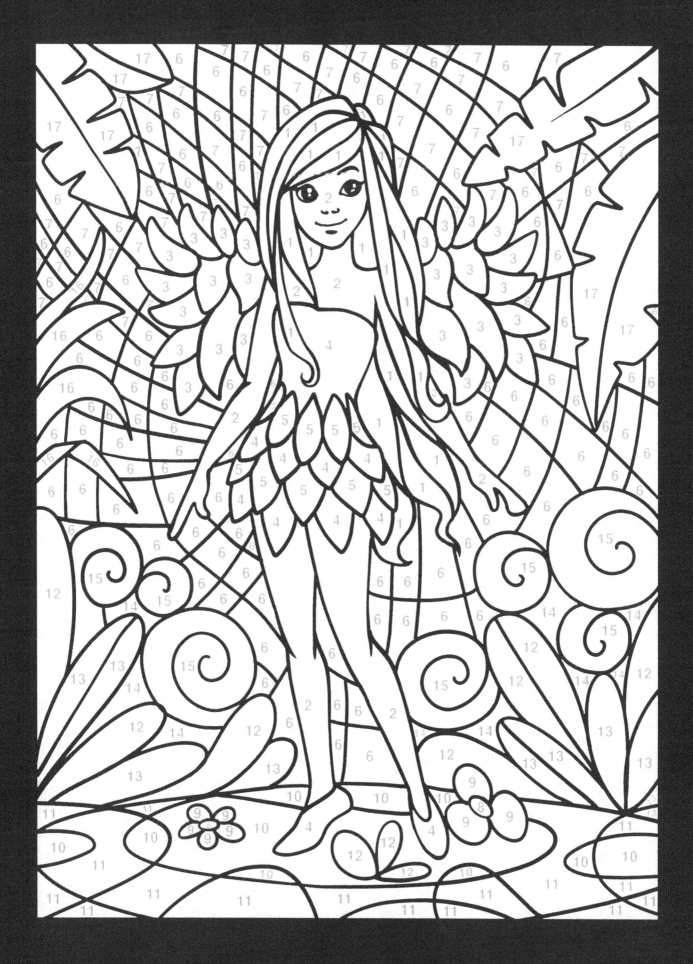

1. Dark Brown
2. Peach
3. Violet
4. Orange
5. Pink
6. Light Pink
7. Light Orange
8. Neon Green
9. Army Green
10. Red
11. Yellow
12. Green
13. Medium Green
14. Dark Green
15. Light Green

16. Light Blue
17. Baby Blue

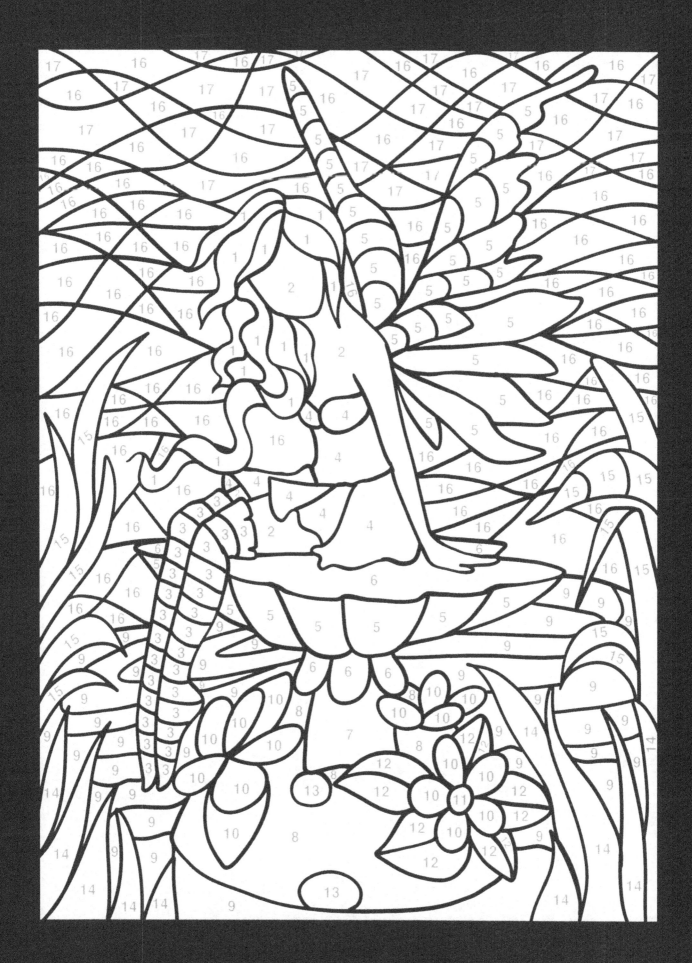

1. Dark Brown
2. Peach
3. Pink
4. Light Pink
5. Violet
6. Orange
7. Light Violet
8. Red
9. Yellow
10. Neon Green
11. Green
12. Dark Green
13. Light Green
14. Brown
15. Dark Orange
16. Light Brown
17. Blue
18. Light Blue

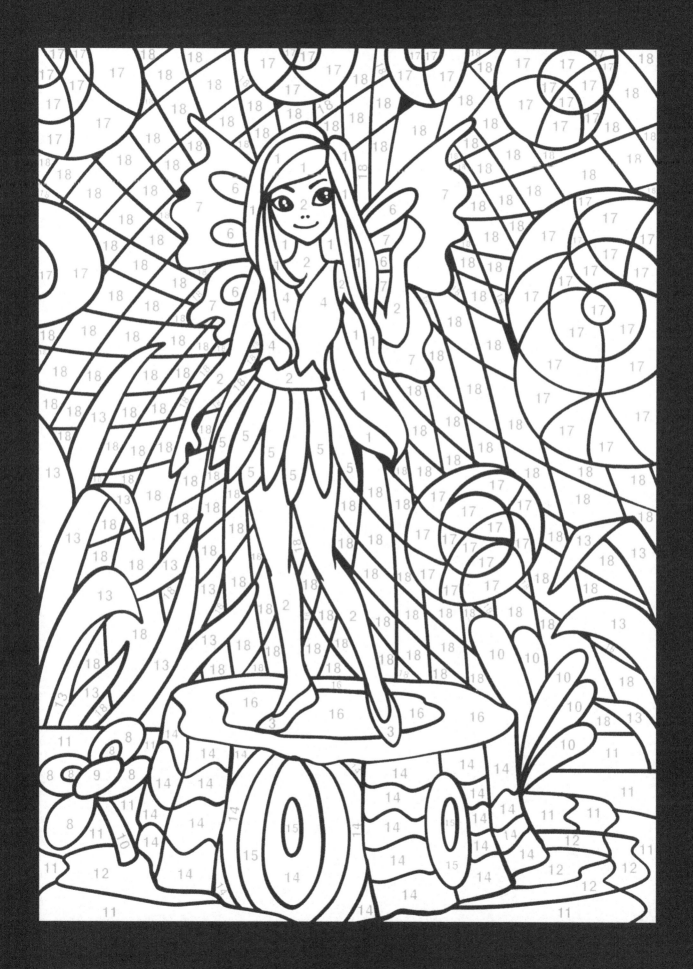

1. Dark Brown
2. Peach
3. Blue
4. Light Violet
5. Dark Violet
6. Violet
7. Light Orange
8. Light Brown
9. Light Blue
10. Yellow
11. Pink
12. Dark Pink
13. Brown
14. Dark Green
15. Green
16. Light Green
17. Neon Green
18. Orange

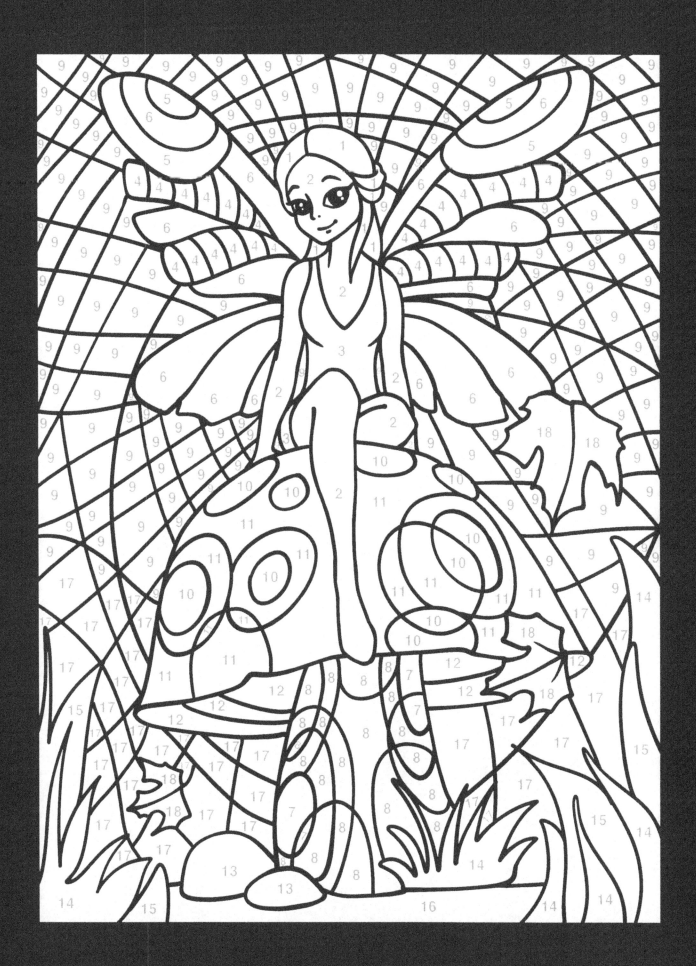

1. Dark Brown

2. Peach

3. Pink

4. Light Pink

5. Orange

6. Dark Green

7. Yellow

8. Army Green

9. Green

10. Medium Green

11. Light Brown

12. Light Orange

13. Red

14. Light Green

15. Neon Green

16. Light Blue

17. Baby Blue

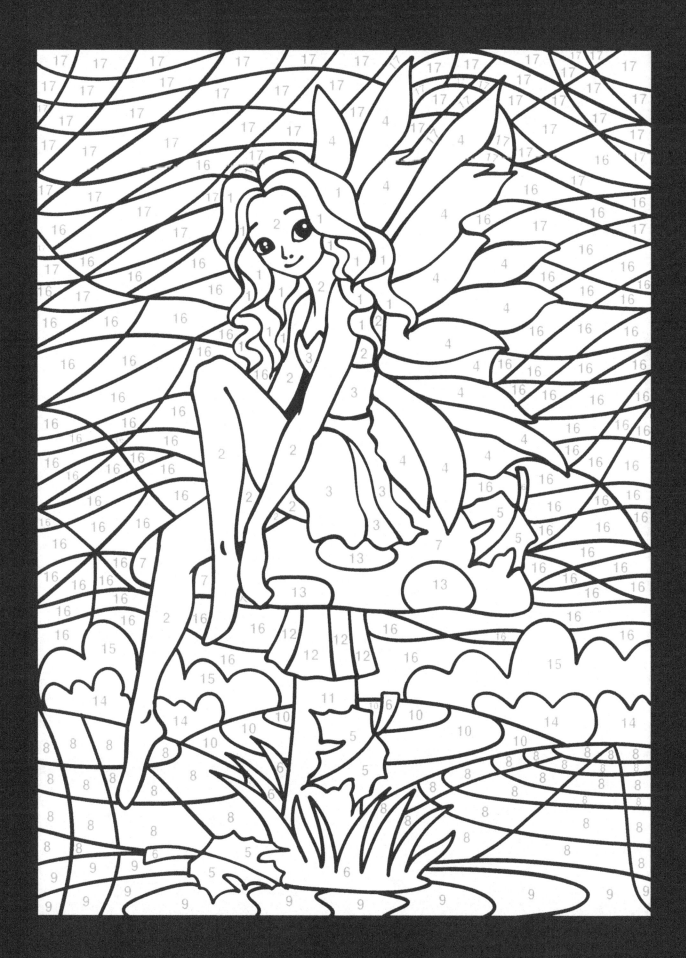

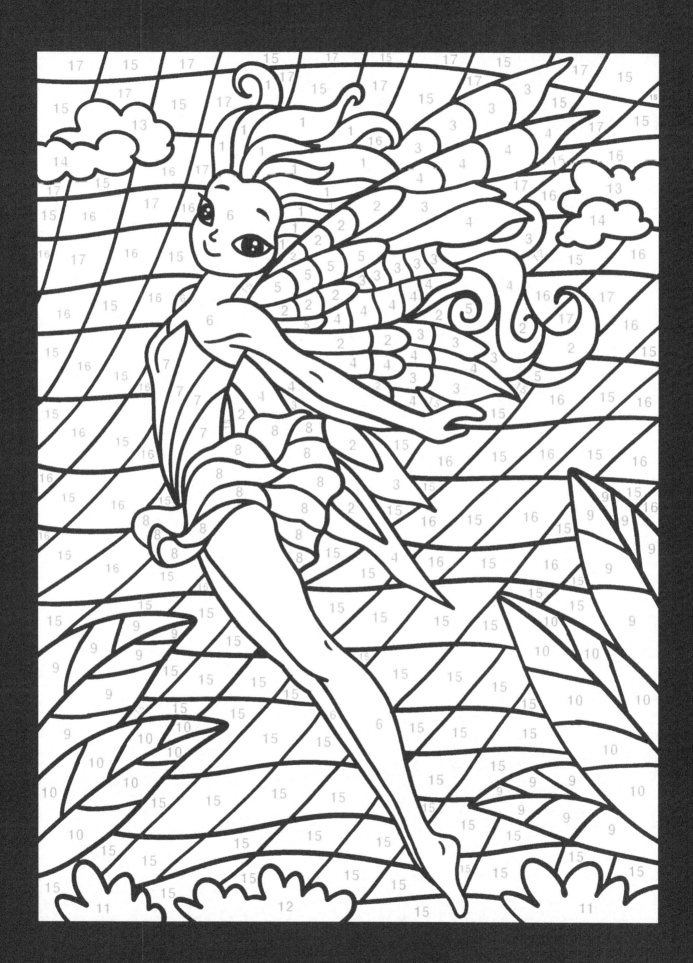

1. Neon Green

2. Light Green

3. Dark Brown

4. Green

5. Yellow

6. Pink

7. Light Pink

8. Dark Brown

9. Brown

10. Light Brown

11. Peach

12. Violet

13. Light Violet

14. Dark Violet

15. Orange

16. Dark Green

17. Light Blue

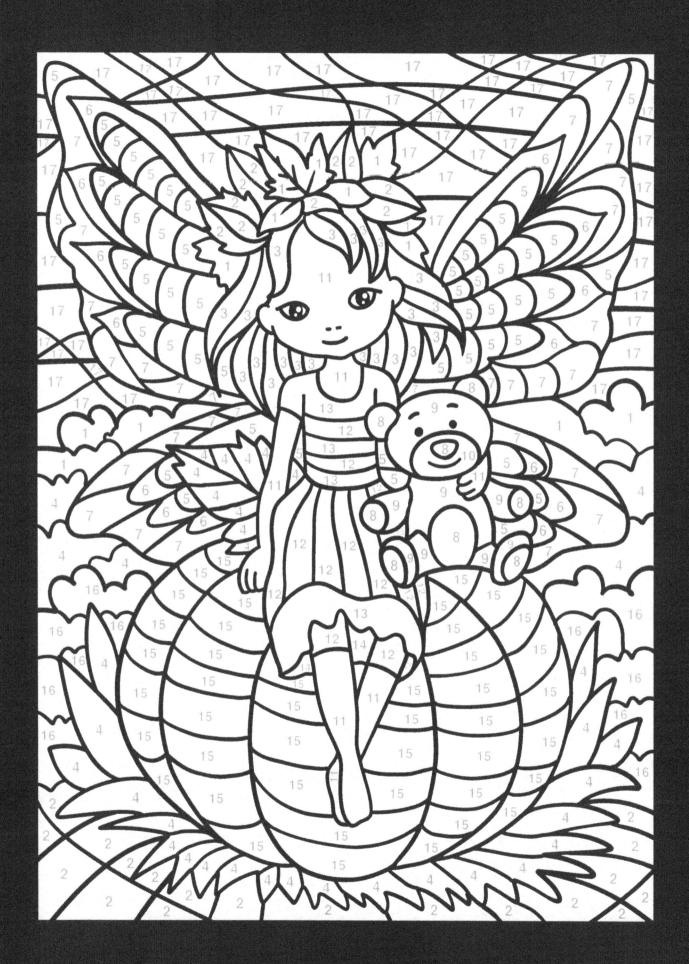

1. Dark Brown
2. Peach
3. Red
4. Dark Red
5. Yellow
6. Violet
7. Orange
8. Light Blue
9. Baby Blue
10. Blue
11. Light Green
12. Green
13. Dark Green
14. Medium Green
15. Pink
16. Neon Green
17. Light Gray

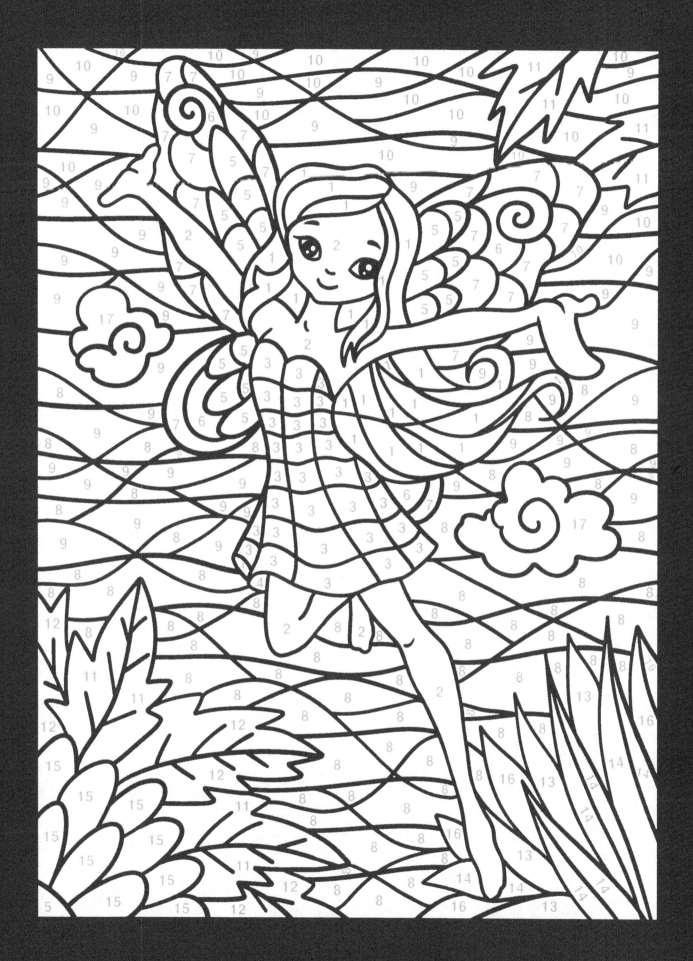

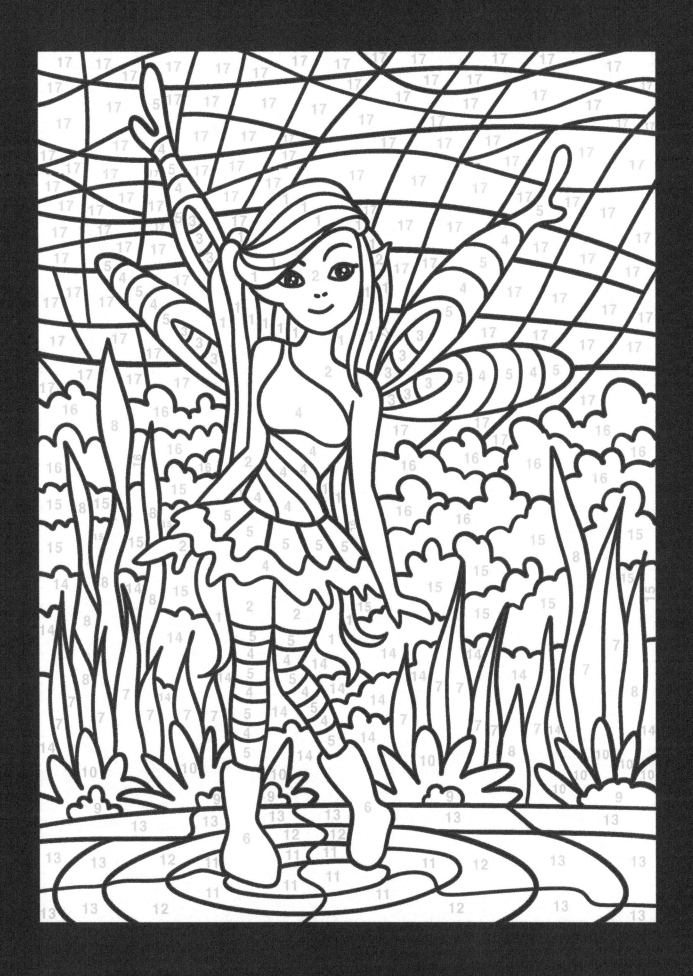

1. Dark Brown
2. Peach
3. Pink
4. Light Pink
5. Yellow
6. Orange
7. Blue
8. Violet
9. Light Violet
10. Light Brown
11. Green
12. Army Green
13. Dark Green
14. Light Green
15. Neon Green
16. Light Blue
17. Baby Blue

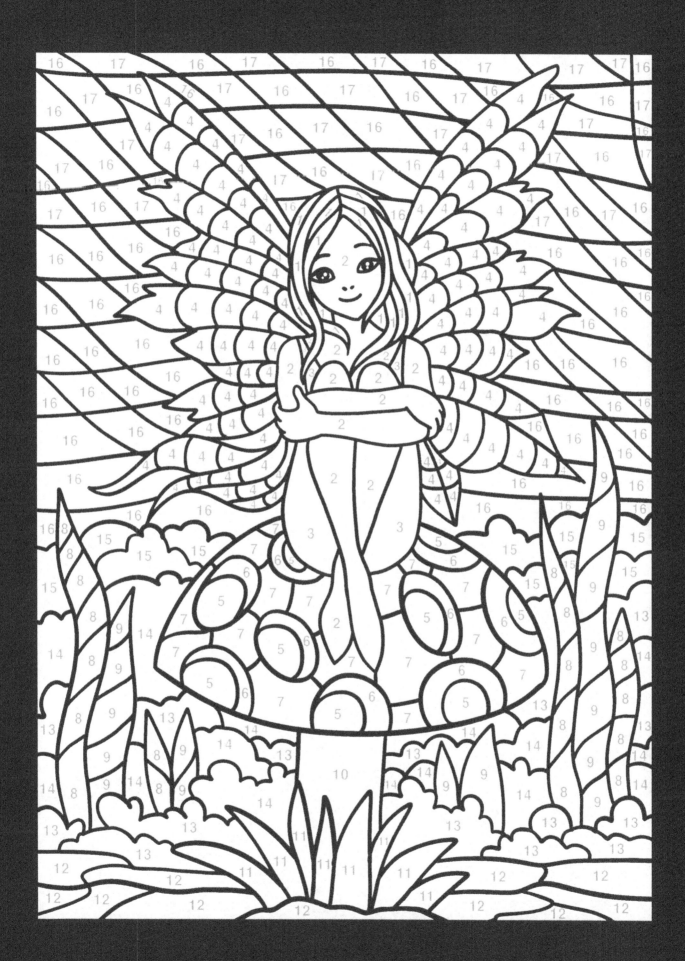

1. Dark Brown
2. Pink
3. Peach
4. Light Green
5. Green
6. Blue
7. Orange
8. Light Pink
9. Violet
10. Light Violet
11. Brown
12. Dark Green
13. Army Green
14. Medium Green
15. Neon Green
16. Light Blue
17. Baby Blue

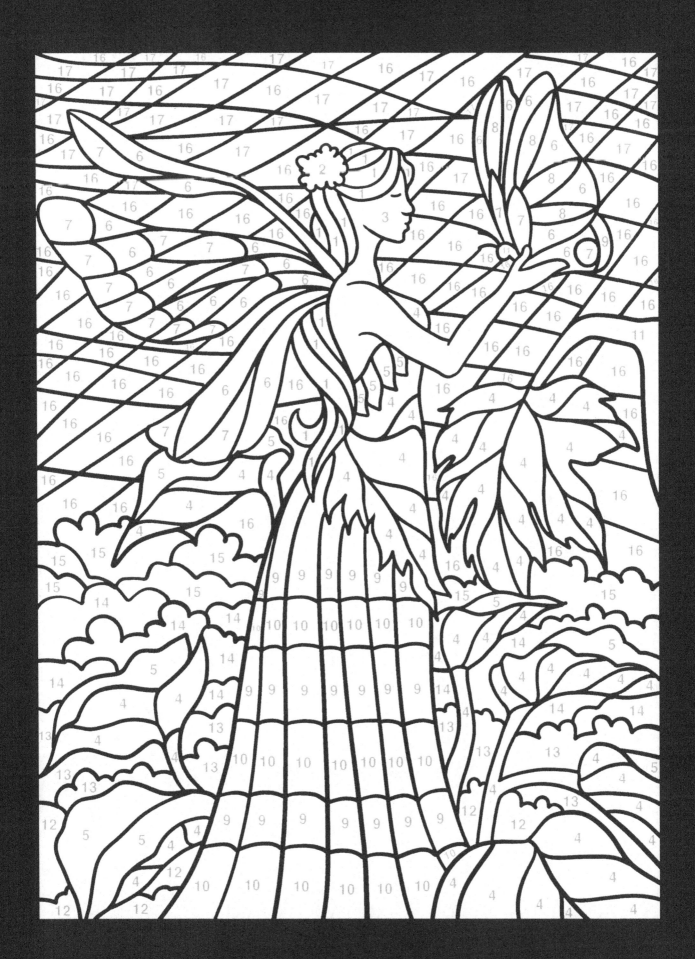

1. Dark Brown
2. Peach
3. Light Pink
4. Pink
5. Violet
6. Dark Violet
7. Light Violet
8. Orange
9. Blue
10. Light Gray
11. Yellow
12. Red
13. Dark Red
14. Light Brown
15. Green
16. Dark Green
17. Light Green
18. Light Blue

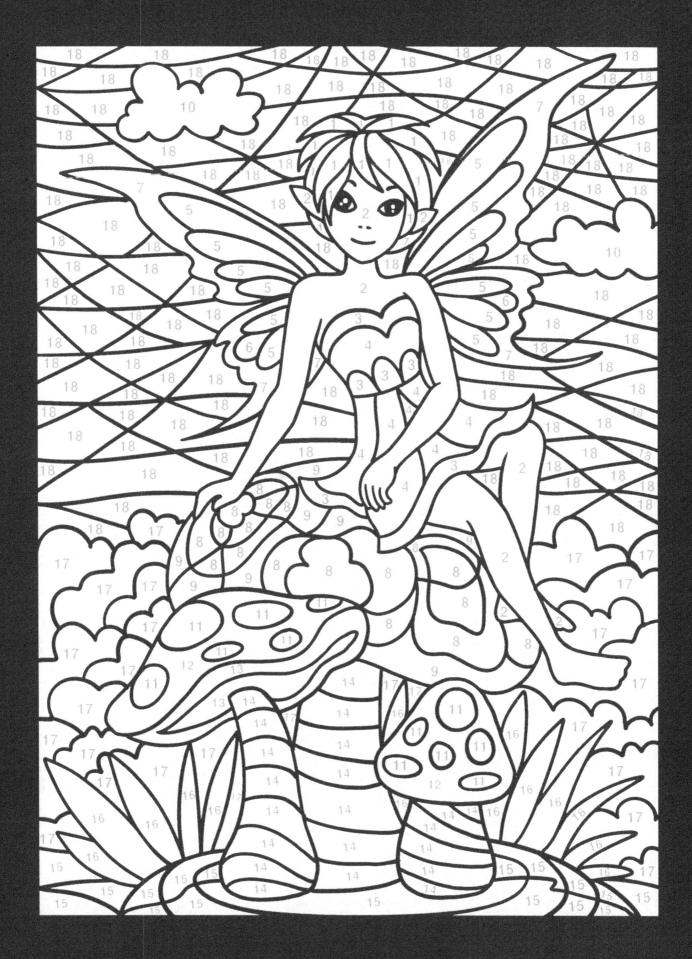

1. Dark Brown
2. Peach
3. Light Violet
4. Violet
5. Yellow
6. Pink
7. Light Pink
8. Green
9. Dark Green
10. Orange
11. Light Orange
12. Red
13. Blue
14. Light Green
15. Neon Green
16. Light Blue
17. Baby Blue

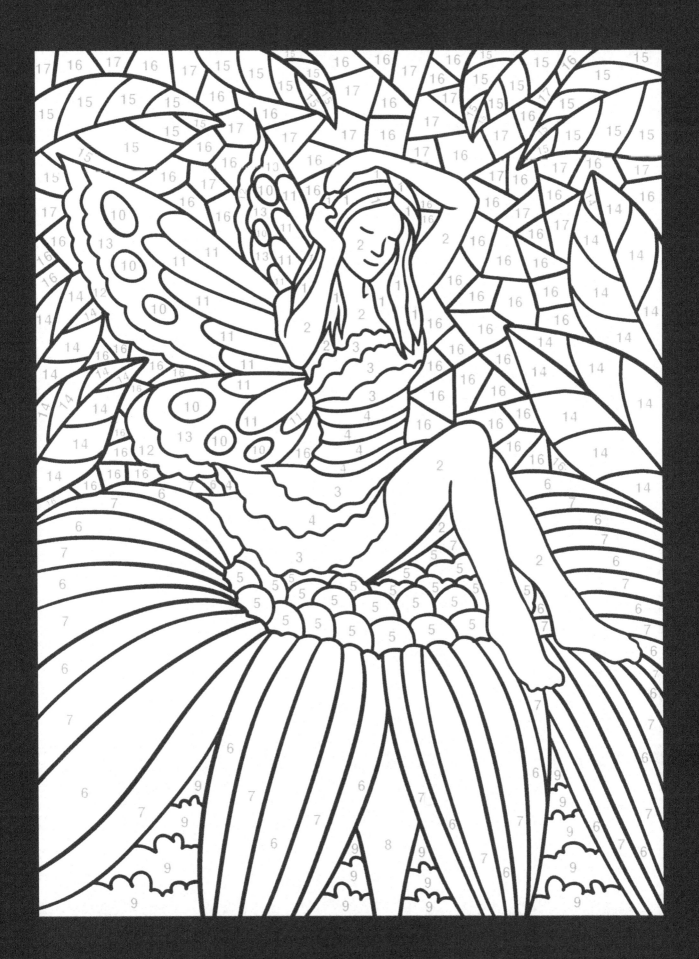

1. Dark Brown
2. Peach
3. Red
4. Yellow
5. Neon Green
6. Green
7. Army Green
8. Orange
9. Blue
10. Light Orange
11. Light Pink
12. Pink
13. Dark Green
14. Light Gray
15. Light Green
16. Light Blue
17. Baby Blue

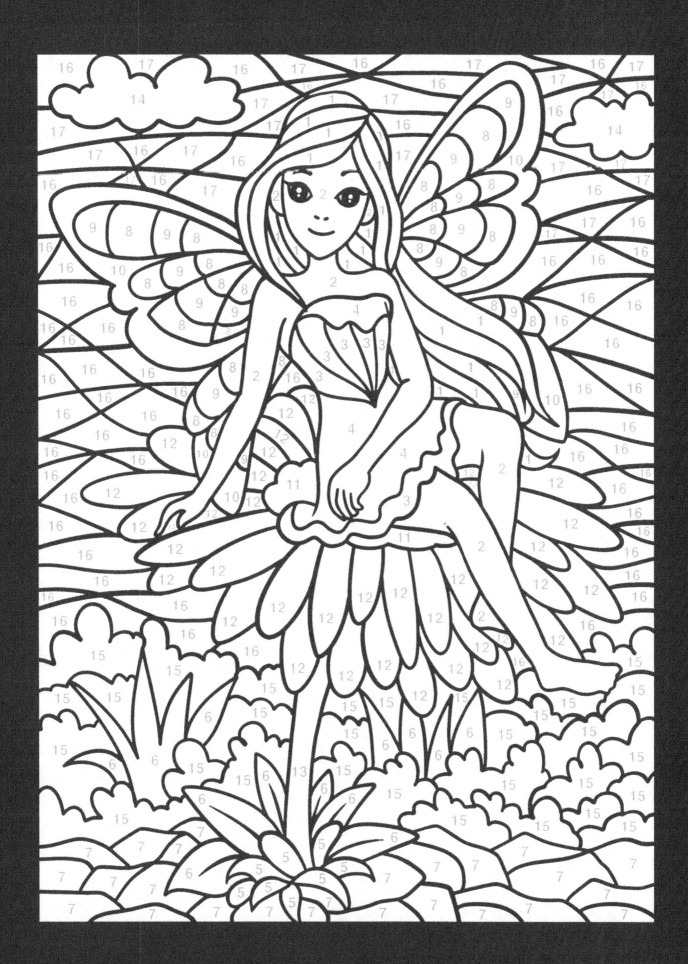

1. Dark Brown

2. Peach

3. Green

4. Blue

5. Orange

6. Pink

7. Dark Pink

8. Light Violet

9. Violet

10. Dark Violet

11. Army Green

12. Light Pink

13. Neon Green

14. Light Green

15. Yellow

16. Red

17. Light Blue

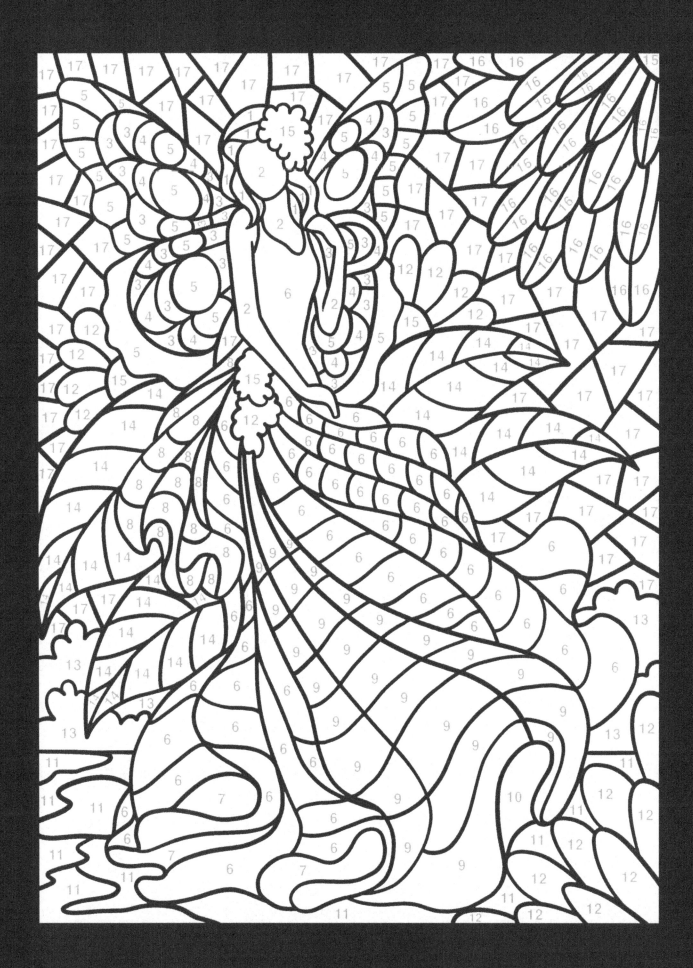

ENJOY BONUS
IMAGES FROM SOME
OF OUR
OTHER FUN
COLOR BY NUMBER
BOOKS!

FIND ALL OF OUR
BOOKS
ON AMAZON

Unicorn
BLACK BACKGROUND
Mosaic Color by Number
Coloring Book

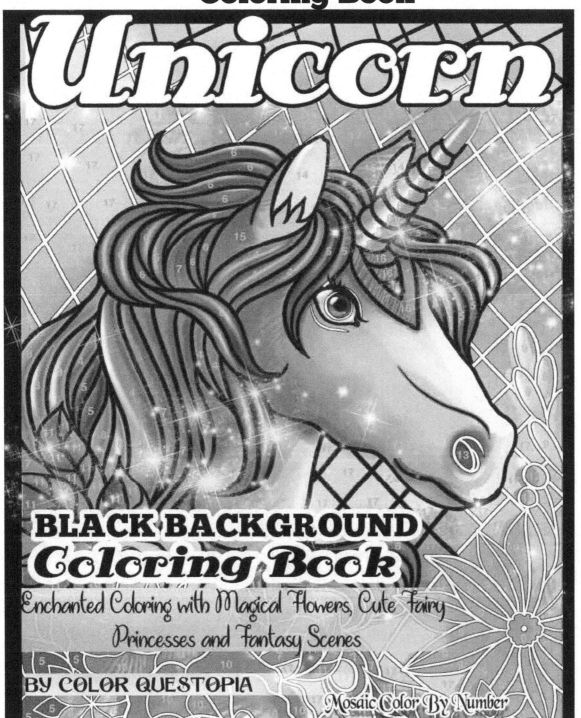

1. Black
2. Blue
3. White
4. Light Violet
5. Violet
6. Yellow
7. Light Pink
8. Orange
9. Red
10. Green
11. Medium Blue
12. Medium Orange
13. Dark Blue
14. Pink
15. Soft Violet
16. Dark Violet
17. Baby Blue

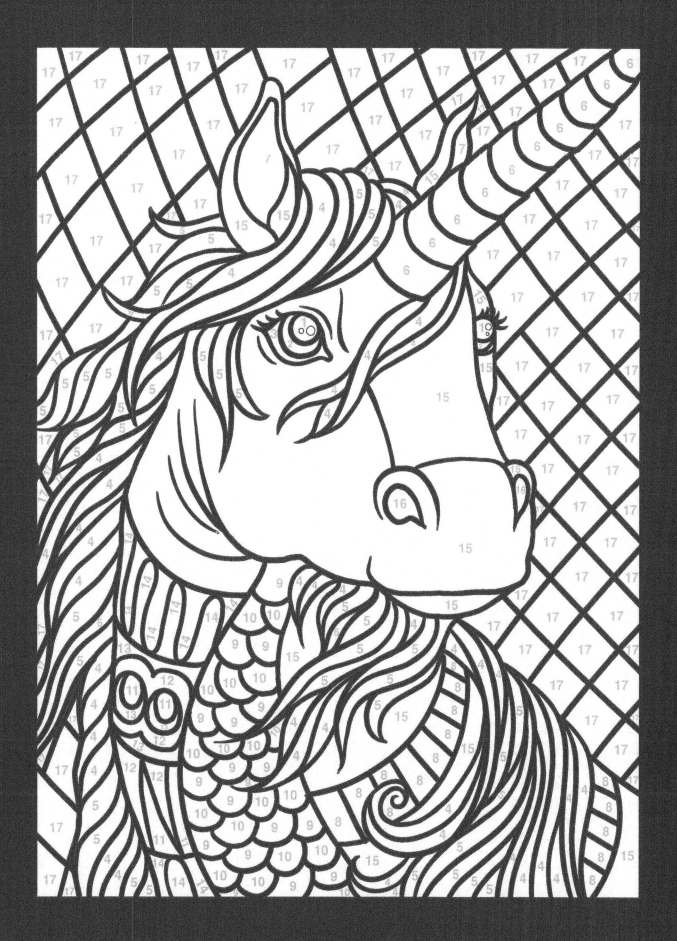

Amazing Owls
BLACK BACKGROUND
Mosaic Color By Number

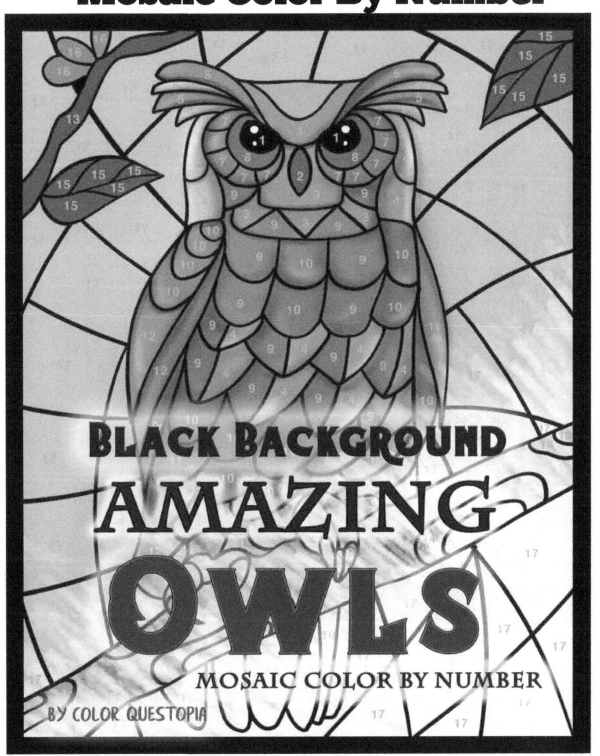

1. Black
2. Blue
3. Orange
4. Light Brown
5. Dark Orange
6. Light Red
7. Yellow
8. Medium Orange
9. Light Orange
10. Dark Yellow
11. Dark Brown
12. Medium Brown
13. Brown
14. Army Green
15. Dark Green
16. Green
17. Sky Blue

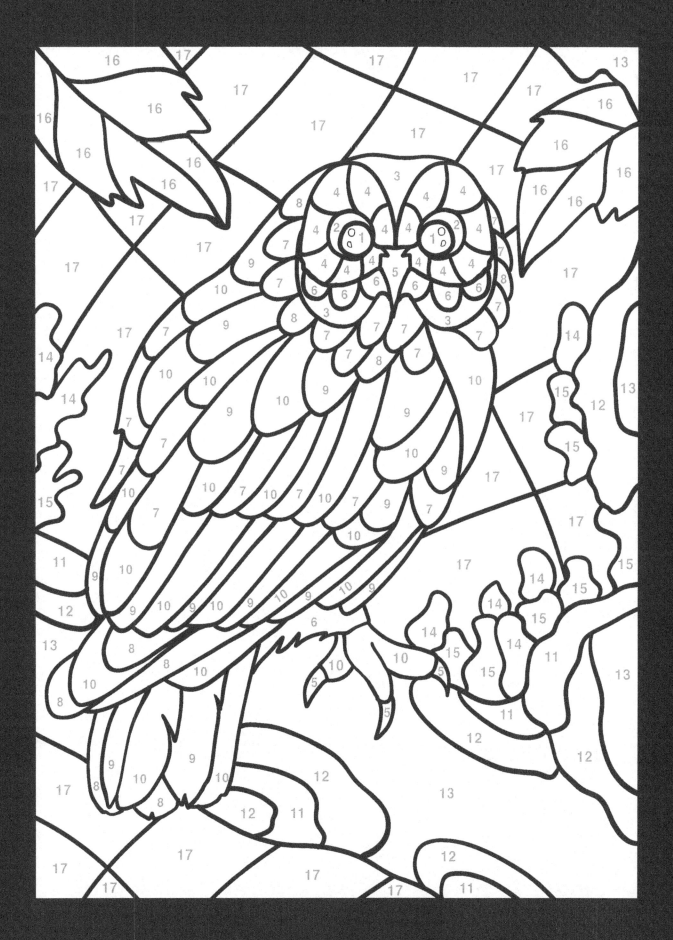

Fantasy Landscapes
BLACK BACKGROUND
Mosaic Color By Number
Coloring Book for Adults

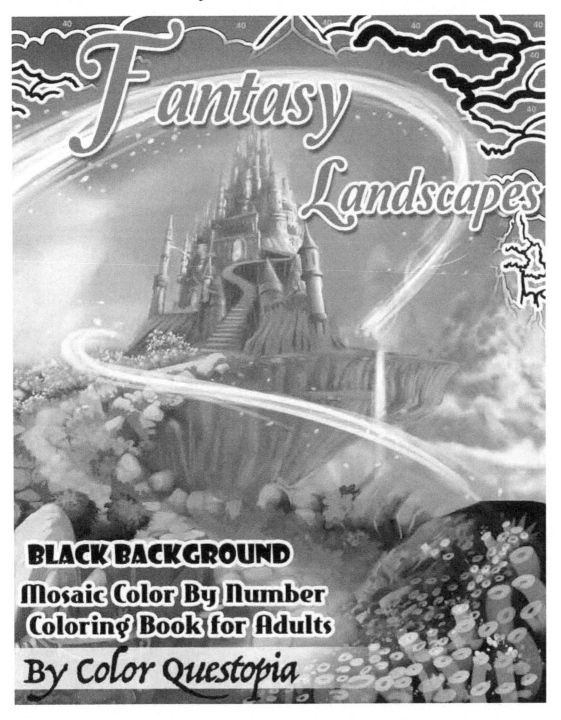

1. Black	26. Dark Green
2. Golden	27. Peach
3. Light Red	28. Light Pink
4. Medium Red	29. Medium Pink
5. Red	30. Pink
6. Dark Red	31. Hot Pink
7. Lemon Yellow	32. Dark Pink
8. Light Yellow	33. Medium Purple
9. Yellow	34. Purple
10. Dark Yellow	35. Light Violet
11. Bright Orange	36. Soft Violet
12. Light Orange	37. Violet
13. Medium Orange	38. Dark Violet
14. Orange	39. Baby Blue
15. Dark Orange	40. Sky Blue
16. Chocolate	41. Light Blue
17. Light Brown	42. Medium Blue
18. Medium Brown	43. Blue
19. Brown	44. Dark Blue
20. Dark Brown	45. Navy Blue
21. Neon Green	46. Beige
22. Light Green	47. Light Gray
23. Medium Green	48. Medium Gray
24. Green	49. Gray
25. Army Green	50. Dark Gray

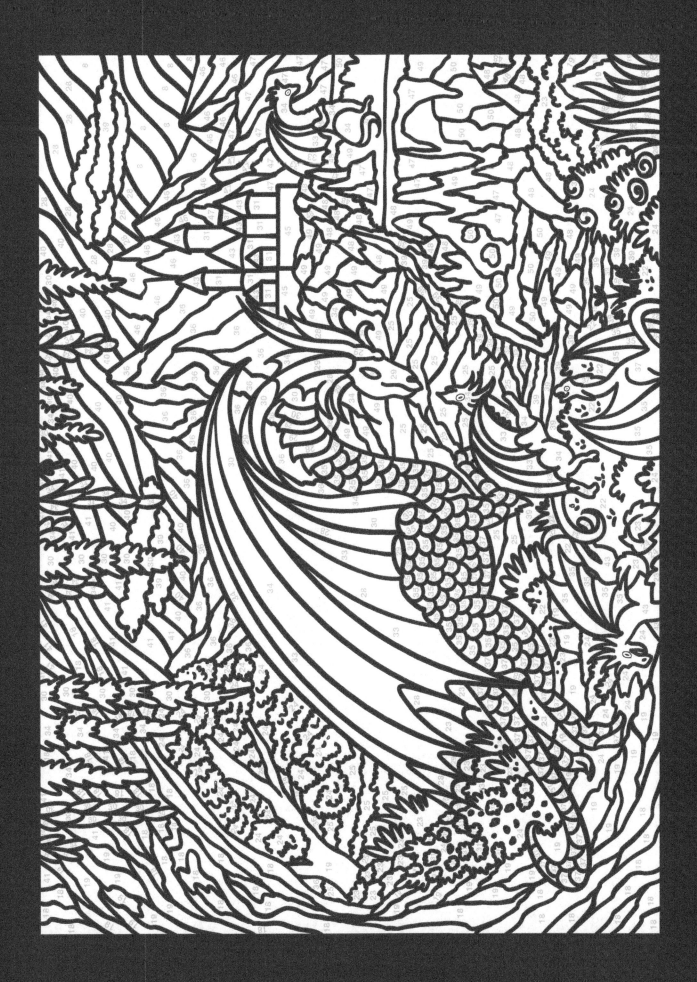

Autumn
BLACK BACKGROUND
Mosaic Adult Color By Numbers
Magical Fall Coloring Book

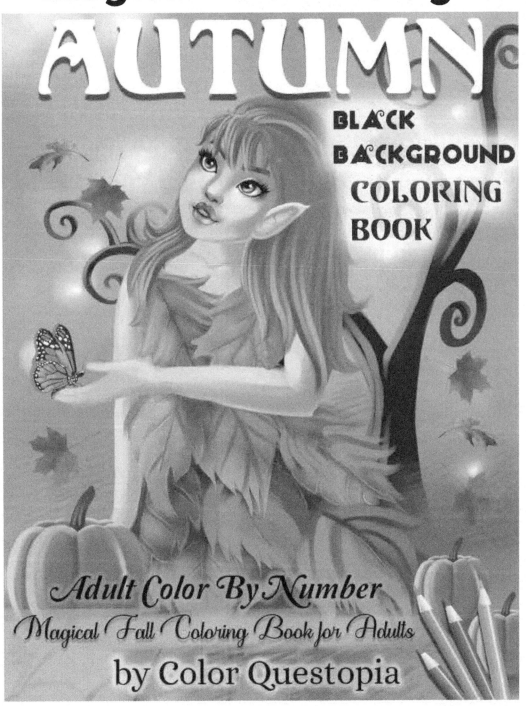

1. Black	26. Dark Green
2. Golden	27. Peach
3. Light Red	28. Light Pink
4. Medium Red	29. Medium Pink
5. Red	30. Pink
6. Dark Red	31. Hot Pink
7. Lemon Yellow	32. Dark Pink
8. Light Yellow	33. Medium Purple
9. Yellow	34. Purple
10. Dark Yellow	35. Light Violet
11. Bright Orange	36. Soft Violet
12. Light Orange	37. Violet
13. Medium Orange	38. Dark Violet
14. Orange	39. Baby Blue
15. Dark Orange	40. Sky Blue
16. Chocolate	41. Light Blue
17. Light Brown	42. Medium Blue
18. Medium Brown	43. Blue
19. Brown	44. Dark Blue
20. Dark Brown	45. Navy Blue
21. Neon Green	46. Beige
22. Light Green	47. Light Gray
23. Medium Green	48. Medium Gray
24. Green	49. Gray
25. Army Green	50. Dark Gray

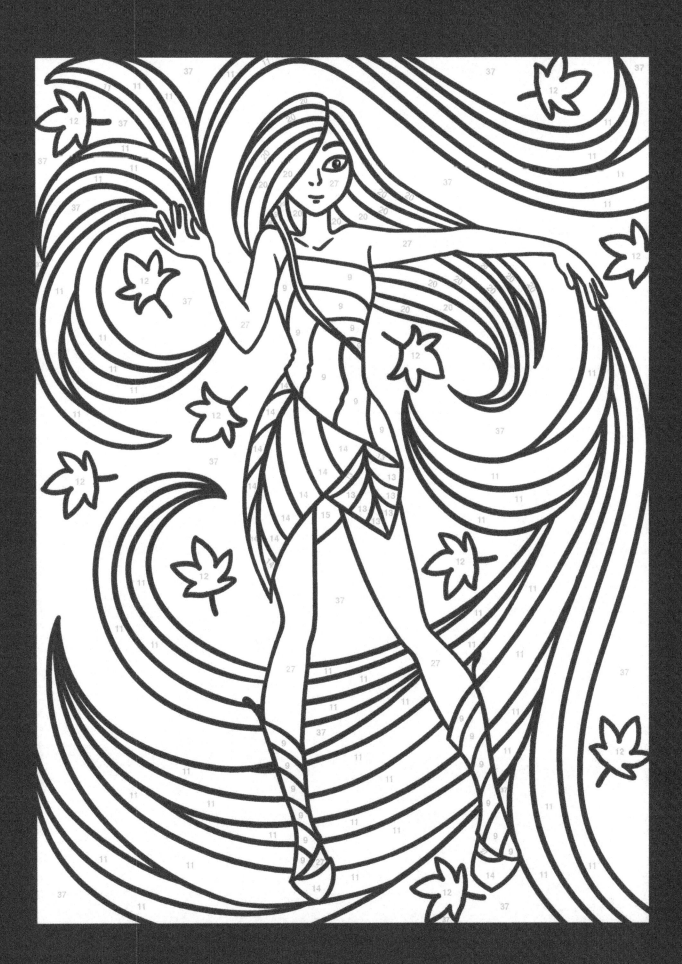

Fashion
BLACK BACKGROUND
Color By Number
Coloring Book For Adults

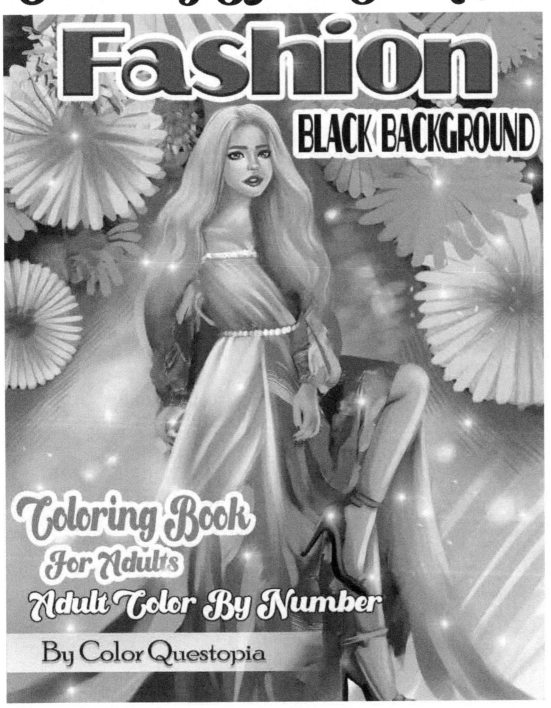

1. Black
2. Golden
3. Light Red
4. Medium Red
5. Red
6. Dark Red
7. Lemon Yellow
8. Light Yellow
9. Yellow
10. Dark Yellow
11. Bright Orange
12. Light Orange
13. Medium Orange
14. Orange
15. Dark Orange
16. Chocolate
17. Light Brown
18. Medium Brown
19. Brown
20. Dark Brown
21. Neon Green
22. Light Green
23. Medium Green
24. Green
25. Army Green
26. Dark Green
27. Peach
28. Light Pink
29. Medium Pink
30. Pink
31. Hot Pink
32. Dark Pink
33. Medium Purple
34. Purple
35. Light Violet
36. Soft Violet
37. Violet
38. Dark Violet
39. Baby Blue
40. Sky Blue
41. Light Blue
42. Medium Blue
43. Blue
44. Dark Blue
45. Navy Blue
46. Beige
47. Light Gray
48. Medium Gray
49. Gray
50. Dark Gray

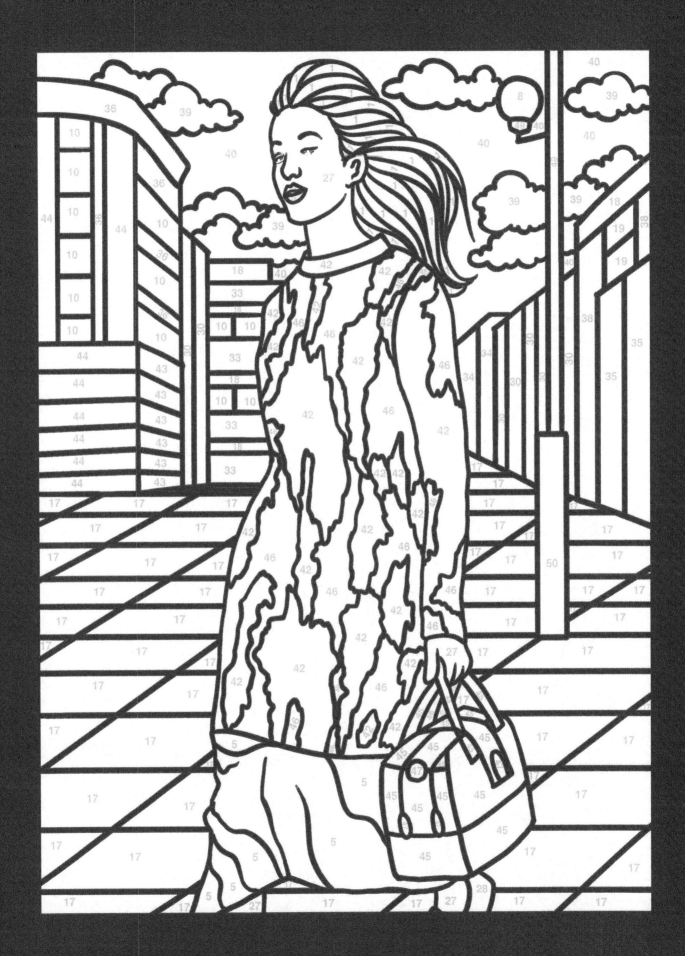

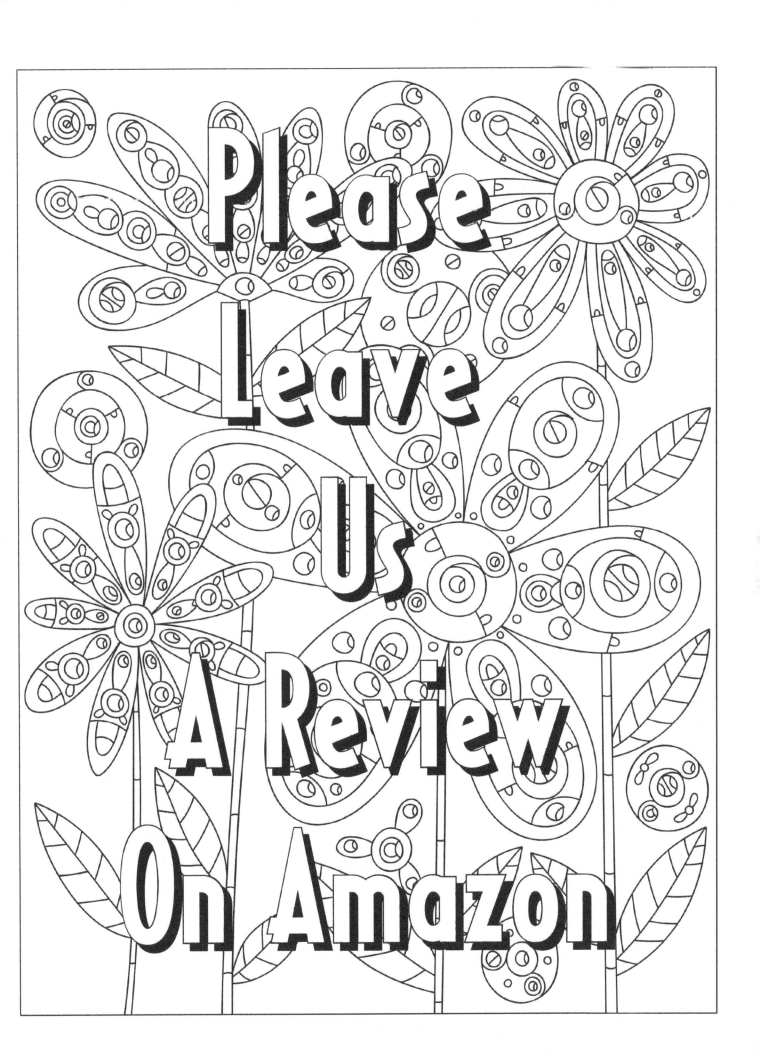

Made in United States
Orlando, FL
11 January 2022

13296149R10039